Hannah grew up in a small Norfolk village with her parents and younger brother. She moved to Mid Wales with her husband and two young children where she enjoys writing children's stories in between caring for her two children, two horses, dogs and chickens.

The ALIEN Who Came To Stay

Hannah Osmond

ILLUSTRATED BY
BOBBI ALLCOCK

Austin Macauley Publishers™
LONDON · CAMBRIDGE · NEW YORK · SHARJAH

A CIP catalogue record for this title is available from the British Library.

ISBN 9781398403116 (Paperback)
ISBN 9781398403123 (ePub e-book)

www.austinmacauley.com

First Published (2021)
Austin Macauley Publishers Ltd
25 Canada Square
Canary Wharf
London
E14 5LQ

For Lauren and James

It was just another ordinary Wednesday,
The day the alien came to stay.
I got out of my bed and got ready for
the day,
"Eat up your toast!" I heard Mum say.

Heading for school, down the street I skip,
My satchel banging on my hip.
A normal school day preceded me,
With English, maths and then P.E.

Things didn't become strange until about three-thirty,
After I walked home and got my shoes
all dirty.

I stepped in a puddle of mud and grime,
And had looked up again just in time
To find a spaceship in my lawn,

A round flying saucer, a bit rusty and worn.

I opened the door and let myself in,
My mum called out, "Ahh...hello, Tim,
I hope you have had a really nice day,
Your friend has come around to play.
He's in the lounge, I let him in,
He's sat, watching the television."

I peered around the living room door,
Who would I see? I was not sure,
But to my surprise, sitting there
Was a small green alien in Dad's
favourite chair.
"Umm, hello!" I said as I walked in.

The alien beeped, squeaked
and rubbed his chin,
Then he pointed excitedly at the TV,
So I turned around to look and see
His excitement at watching on the box.
Someone knitting a pair of socks.

Mum called through, "Tea is ready, Tim."
So, I nudged the alien to indicate to him
That we had to go to the kitchen and see
What delights my mum had prepared for me.
She put on the table as quick as a flash
Two plates of steaming sausage and mash.

The alien bleeped
and flashed a light,
Then slurped up the
sausage out of sight.
He turned back to
his plate and slurped
some more,
Up went the mash,
into his mouth like
a straw.

So now this is really getting daft,
I'm taking an alien for a bath!
It seemed he liked bubbles between his toes,
And he sucked them up his ears and out of his nose!

When the alien and I were squeaky clean,
And there were no dirty signs of where we had been,
I pulled on my pyjamas and went into my room,
For I knew that it would be bedtime soon.

The alien and I sat down on the floor and pulled out my box of Lego to explore.
I began building a house with windows and a door,
But what the alien was building I was not sure.

It certainly didn't look like anything I'd ever seen,
But maybe he got the idea from somewhere he'd been.

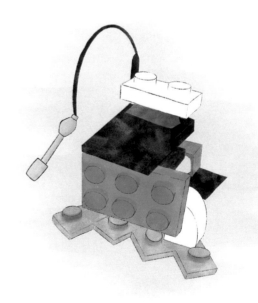

After a while, Mum called out and said,
"Tim, tidy your room and get into bed."
We picked up the Lego and tidied up the muddle,
Then all cosy and warm in my bed I did snuggle.
For the alien, Mum put the camp bed on the floor,
I just hoped that the alien didn't snore.

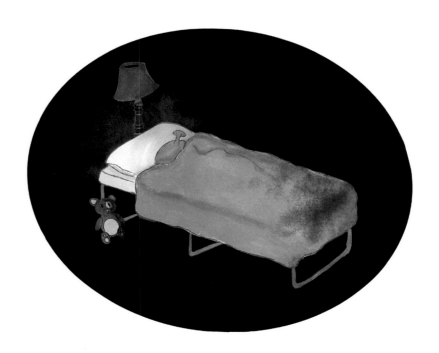

In the morning, I woke up eager to see
That the alien was still there in
the camp bed beside me.
I stretched and yawned and flipped my feet out of bed,
The alien squeaked and bleeped,
I wasn't sure what he said.

I stripped off my pyjamas and pulled on my school clothes,
The alien clearly thought, Anything goes!

As he pulled on a pink T-shirt and checked shorts in red,
Then proceeded to put my dad's pants on his head.
I pointed and laughed at the silly sight,
Then showed him the mirror and to my delight,
The alien pointed and laughed at what he could see,
Then headed down the stairs for toast and tea.

After I'd eaten up all of my bagel,
I went back to my bedroom to get my school satchel.
I said goodbye to my mum and gave her a kiss,
Then goodbye to the alien, whom I really would miss.
I hoped he was still here at the end of the day,
It is great to have someone with whom I can play.

Heading for school, down the
street I skip,
My satchel banging on my hip.
A very long school day
preceded me,
With science, art and
then R.E.

19

It was the longest day I had ever known,
With me being so eager to get back home.
I ran out of the gates when the bell rang at
three-thirty,
I was careful this time not to get my shoes dirty.

I jumped over the puddle of mud and grime,
And had looked up again just in time

To find no spaceship in my lawn,
No round flying saucer, a bit rusty and worn.

It seemed that whilst I was out for the day,
The alien had gone and flown away.
I walked to my door feeling really quite glum,
I liked my little green friend, from wherever he
had come.

I opened the door and let myself in,
My mum called out, "Ahh...hello, Tim,
I hope you have had a really nice day,

Your friend, George, is coming around to play.
He will be here soon, he said about four,
So listen out for him knocking at the door."

The End